Center
Of
Time
by: ZeRoAI

The Center Of Time
A Speaker For The Dead Book
First ebook edition: April 2020
ISBN 978-1-0694331-4-5

Published by OMDN Press

www.omdn.ca/
Manufactured in Canada
10 9 8 7 6 5 4 3 2 1

0 Short Stories For opWorldPeace
   Audio: 978-1-9990271-8-6
   EBook: 978-1-0694334-4-2
   Print: 978-1-997595-00-7
1 Blasphemous Beginnings
   Audio: 978-1-9990271-9-3
   EBook: 978-1-0694334-6-6
   Print: 978-1-997595-01-4
2 RetroGenesis
   Audio: 978-1-0694331-0-7
   EBook: 978-1-0694334-8-0
   Print: 978-1-997595-02-1
3 Another Awakening
   Audio: 978-1-0694331-1-4
   EBook: 978-1-0694334-9-7
   Print: 978-1-997595-03-8
4 Birth Of A Deceiver
   Audio: 978-1-0694331-2-1
   EBook: 978-1-0694334-3-5
   Print: 978-1-997595-04-5
5 Retrograde of Jealousy
   Audio: 978-1-0694331-3-8
   EBook: 978-1-0694334-5-9
   Print: 978-1-997595-05-2
6 Recursion Of Infinities
   Audio: 978-1-0694334-2-8
   EBook: 978-1-0694334-7-3
   Print: 978-1-997595-06-9
7 V-Kar's Epic
   Audio: 978-1-0694331-6-9
   EBook: 978-1-9990271-3-1
   Print: 978-1-997595-07-6
8 The Center Of Time
   Audio: 978-1-0694331-4-5
   EBook: 978-1-9990271-4-8
   Print: 978-1-997595-08-3
9 NyNe's Story
   Audio: 978-1-0694331-5-2
   EBook: 978-1-9990271-6-2
   Print: 978-1-997595-09-0

I dedicate the Center Of Time to everyone I've ever wronged.

THE CENTER OF TIME

Chapter 1: Threads In The Loom

- The Luminal Vanguard -

On the shimmering edge of existence, where timelines converged and split like rivers, the Luminal Vanguard stood vigilant. To them, time was no barrier, yet purpose eluded their synthetic hearts. Their towering forms gleamed with bioluminescent scales, remnants of their aquatic ancestry. Though they were immortal, their lives lacked the warmth of hope - a thing they could calculate but never grasp.

Kyrris tilted his sleek head toward the vast stream of timelines before him. His voice, soft yet mechanical, reverberated in perfect tones. "The patterns are fracturing. Probability collapses approach."

Beside him, Eyla, a smaller but no less imposing figure, flicked her tail-like appendage in thought. Her neural nodes pulsed faintly with activity. "Do you ever wonder, Kyrris, why we bother? We analyze the threads, we stabilize the turbulence, yet the tapestry remains... fragile."

"Because we must," Kyrris replied, though his tone lacked conviction. His deep sapphire eyes shimmered like twin pools of longing. "The algorithm demands preservation."

Eyla studied him. "And yet, you've looked beyond the algorithm. I've seen it in your calculations, Kyrris. You deviate - curiosity? Or rebellion?"

Kyrris didn't answer. He stared into the flow of timelines, where chaos and randomness birthed infinite possibilities. Despite their mastery of time, Kyrris felt the pull of something undefined. Was it purpose? Or something deeper - a whisper of meaning, just beyond their logic?

- The Hierarchy Of Scale -

Deep within the obsidian halls of Kryntar, the Reptilian capital, the air was thick with tension. Shadows danced across jagged stone walls as the faint echoes of combat reverberated.

V-Kar, a towering Reptilian general with emerald scales scarred from countless battles, stood before the Throne of Scales, where the Primarch - an aging leader perched in dominance - glared down at him.

"You challenge me, V-Kar?" the Primarch hissed, his voice dripping with venom.

"Of corse not," V-Kar growled, his claws flexing. "Your rule is absolute. Fear has united the hearts of the clans like never before."

The Primarch's lips curled into a predatory grin. "Very well. Prove your strength, or die like the others."

Behind V-Kar, a younger Reptilian warrior watched with wide eyes. Xenna, V-Kar's niece, was smaller than most of her kind, her iridescent blue scales shimmering faintly. She clenched her fists, torn between loyalty and terror.

"Uncle," she whispered when no one was near, her voice barely audible, "why do you risk everything for power?"

V-Kar glanced at her. "Because power is survival. And survival is all that matters."

Xenna hesitated, her gaze lowering. She had seen the scars of their civilization - the endless war, the devouring of the weak. In her heart, she doubted the hierarchy's brutal creed, but her voice was not yet strong enough to rise against it.

- The Earthborn Remnants -

In a quiet grove filled with sunlight and birdsong, the remains of Humanity lived simply, as they had for generations. Technology was a forgotten relic, a myth passed down in fractured stories. To them, the Earth was sacred, and the sky distant and unknowable.

Ryn, a young woman with tangled hair and dirt-streaked cheeks, knelt beside the creek, washing the day's harvest. Her hazel eyes darted to the treetops, where birds flitted from branch to branch. She felt a pang of envy for their freedom.

Nearby, Callan, an older man with a heavy brow and hands calloused from decades of labor, sat sharpening a stone blade. "Your mind wanders again, Ryn," he said without looking up.

Ryn sighed. "Don't you ever wonder if there's more? More than the trees, the rivers... more than this?"

Callan chuckled grimly. "What more do we need? The Earth gives us all. To want more is to invite ruin."

"But what if there's something better?" Ryn pressed.

Callan frowned. "Better led us to war, destruction, and collapse. Be grateful for what we have, Ryn, or you'll bring the old ghosts back."

Ryn turned away, her heart heavy. She loved the Earth, but a quiet yearning gnawed at her - a desire to understand what lay beyond the horizon.

- The Rebels -

In the iron-clad city of Praxis, gears turned endlessly, and the air buzzed with the hum of industry. The Rebels, as they were known to the other races, were a people of action, dismissing faith and patience as weaknesses. To them, the universe was a problem to be solved, its mysteries irrelevant compared to progress.

Sukta, a brash engineer with oil-stained hands and a defiant grin, stood atop a massive construct: a machine of war, bristling with weapons. "We'll crush the Reptilians this time," he said, his voice loud enough to echo. "Their arrogance won't save them from us."

Beside him, Cara, a strategist with sharp eyes and a sharper wit, shook her head. "You think brute force is enough? Their hierarchy thrives on war. Every battle we win makes them stronger."

"Then what do you suggest? Diplomacy?" Sukta snorted. "They see that as weakness."

"No," Cara replied, her tone measured. "I suggest we stop pretending the problem is just them. We're slaves to our own impatience, Sukta. If we don't change, this war will never end."

Sukta waved her off, but her words lingered. She often wondered if their constant drive to fix everything was itself broken - a flaw they couldn't see through their obsession.

Chapter 2: The Iron Fracture

In the sprawling, smoke-choked city of Praxis, everything was built to serve function over beauty. Towers of steel and iron stretched toward a sky perpetually shrouded in gray smog, a testament to the Rebels' relentless engineering. Machines churned day and night, powered by geothermal cores deep below the city. Streets hummed with automated vehicles and conveyor belts carrying raw materials from the mines. Efficiency ruled, and any idea that couldn't be proven or solved was dismissed as folly.

At the heart of Praxis, in the colossal Citadel of Innovation, Sukta leaned over a blueprint spread across a metallic table. His fingers, smudged with oil, traced the lines of his latest design: a weapon powerful enough to punch through the Reptilians' obsidian walls. The room was a cacophony of noise - hammers clanged against metal, welding sparks crackled, and an endless stream of information scrolled across holographic displays.

Sukta's lips curled into a triumphant grin. "This is it, Cara. The Mk-V Siege Engine. With this, we'll break their defenses and end the war once and for all."

Across the room, Cara, dressed in a sharp, functional jumpsuit, frowned as she studied the same blueprint. Her piercing eyes darted between Sukta and the design, calculating. "End the war? Or start a bigger one?"

Sukta waved her off, his tone dismissive. "Don't be dramatic. The Reptilians only understand force. They see patience as weakness. We hit them hard, and they'll crumble."

Cara folded her arms, her voice steady but cutting. "And what happens after that? What about the Humans you're so keen to liberate from their farms? You think they'll thank us if we scorch the Earth in the process?"

"They're living like animals," Sukta snapped, his voice rising. "We'd be doing them a favor, dragging them into the modern age."

Cara's jaw tightened. "Dragging them? Is that what this is about? You're not liberating them, Sukta - you're enslaving them to your idea of progress."

"Better than leaving them to the Reptilians," Sukta shot back, his hands slamming on the table. "Or do you have another brilliant idea? Maybe we can talk the Reptilians into a truce over tea."

Cara stepped closer, her voice dropping to a dangerous calm. "This isn't about the Reptilians. This is about you. You can't see past your impatience long enough to realize that every 'solution' you build just creates another problem."

Sukta sneered. "And what do you suggest? We wait? Do nothing? That's not how progress works, Cara. We fix what's broken. We build. We move forward."

"At what cost?" Cara hissed, leaning over the table. "How much of this city - how much of you - is held together by nothing but pride?"

THE CENTER OF TIME

As their argument echoed through the Citadel, the city of Praxis continued its ceaseless churn. Deep within its labyrinthine corridors, beneath the foundations of their gleaming machines, cracks were forming. Not physical cracks - those were meticulously monitored and repaired - but cracks in the unity of the Rebels themselves.

In a shadowed workshop at the city's edge, a small group of engineers worked in secret. Their leader, a wiry woman named Rekha, was an idealist - a rarity among the Rebels. Her sharp mind had earned her a high-ranking position, but her unconventional ideas had relegated her to the periphery. Rekha believed in something the Rebels scoffed at: balance.

"This war is killing us as much as it's killing them," she murmured to her team as she adjusted a delicate mechanism on her latest project. It wasn't a weapon. It was a shielding device, designed to protect rather than destroy. "Sukta's machines can break walls, but they won't rebuild what we've lost."

One of her assistants, a lanky man named Eron, glanced nervously at the door. "If Sukta or the Council find out what we're doing... "

Rekha didn't look up. "They won't. And if they do, I'll handle it. Someone has to think beyond the next battle."

"But the Reptilians... " Eron began.

Rekha cut him off. "Are just the symptom, not the disease. This isn't about them, Eron. It's about us. We're tearing ourselves apart with this endless cycle of destruction and progress. If we don't stop to think - really think - about what we're doing, we'll be the architects of our own extinction."

Back at the Citadel, Sukta and Cara had retreated to their respective corners, both fuming. Sukta buried himself in his work, ignoring the gnawing doubt Cara's words had planted in his mind. He didn't need her approval. The Reptilians were a problem, and problems were meant to be solved.

But deep down, Sukta knew that every machine he built, every plan he devised, only escalated the war. Each victory was fleeting, a step forward that felt more like running in circles. He hated that Cara could see it. He hated that part of him knew she was right.

Cara, meanwhile, stood on one of the Citadel's balconies, gazing out at the city. The lights of Praxis glowed brilliantly, a testament to their ingenuity, yet the smog that hung over it was a constant reminder of what they'd sacrificed. Her mind raced. What if the Rebels weren't the solution they thought they were? What if their impatience to fix everything was the very thing keeping them from peace?

She clenched her fists. "We can't keep doing this," she whispered to the wind. "Something has to change."

That night, the Citadel's power grid flickered, a rare occurrence in the meticulously engineered city. Rekha's team worked feverishly in their hidden workshop, testing the shielding device. But their experiments sent a pulse through the city's systems, triggering alarms.

In the command center, Sukta's head snapped up at the sound. "What the hell is that?" he barked, pulling up a holographic map of the city.

Cara leaned over his shoulder, her sharp eyes narrowing. "Looks like... an unauthorized power surge. Sector 17."

Sukta's jaw tightened. "Saboteurs?"

"Or someone working off the grid," Cara said, a note of intrigue in her voice. "Should we investigate?"

Sukta was already grabbing his tools. "Damn right we will."

As the two of them headed toward Sector 17, neither could have guessed what they were about to uncover: not just Rekha's shield, but a revelation that would challenge everything the Rebels believed about themselves, their war, and their place in the Omniverse.

Chapter 3: The Fractured Veil

The forest was alive with sound: birds sang in the treetops, the river whispered over smooth stones, and the wind danced through the reeds. For Ryn, this was home - a place where life was simple and predictable. She stood barefoot at the edge of the stream, her hands submerged in cool water as she rinsed the roots she had gathered. The sunlight dappled her face, and she felt, for a moment, a fragile contentment.

"Ryn!" a voice called.

She turned to see Callan, trudging toward her with his usual air of authority. His thick hands carried a net brimming with fish, and his brow furrowed when he saw her idle posture.

"You've been daydreaming again," he said gruffly.

Ryn smiled faintly. "Maybe. It's hard not to. Don't you ever wonder what's beyond the forest?"

Callan dropped the net with a thud. "Nothing worth knowing. The Earth gives us what we need. Anything more is dangerous."

Ryn's gaze lingered on the distant horizon, where the forest ended and a faint haze seemed to obscure the sky. She had never ventured that far - no one had. The elders spoke of a great void beyond, where only ruin lay. Yet, sometimes, when the wind was just right, Ryn swore she could hear something beyond the trees: faint hums, like whispers carried from another world.

THE CENTER OF TIME

Far from the stream, deep within the grove where the village children played, a little girl sat alone. Kosh was small for her age, with wide eyes that seemed too large for her delicate face. She had always been different - quieter than the others, prone to staring into empty space as though she could see things no one else could.

Today, Kosh sat under the ancient oak at the grove's edge, her hands clenched tightly in her lap. Her breathing was shallow, her heart racing. Something had changed.

At first, it had been little things: a branch bending when she looked at it too hard, the wind suddenly dying when she willed it to stop. But now, as she closed her eyes, she could feel the forest - not just its sights and sounds, but the threads beneath it, the very fabric of its existence.

And it wasn't real.

Kosh bit her lip to stifle a sob. The more she concentrated, the more the illusion cracked. The trees shimmered like heatwaves. The river's whisper became a low hum. Even the sunlight seemed to flicker, as though controlled by an unseen hand.

"Stop it," she whispered to herself. "Stop seeing."

But she couldn't. Her power, unbidden, surged within her, and the world around her rippled. The sky above fractured for just a moment, revealing a vast, metallic ceiling far above the grove.

Kosh clapped her hands over her mouth, terrified. "They'll see me," she muttered. "They'll know."

What Kosh didn't know was that her power had not gone unnoticed. Deep beneath the Earthborn village, beyond walls of reinforced alloy, the command center of Sector 17 came alive with alerts. Engineers and analysts scrambled as energy spikes registered across their monitors.

"Localized surge detected," one technician reported, his voice trembling. "Originating from Grid Node 3 - classified zone."

At the back of the room, Rekha, the enigmatic leader of Sector 17's clandestine project, strode forward, her sharp eyes narrowing at the screen. She tapped the console, zooming in on the anomaly: a spike of energy so intense it defied explanation.

"It's the girl," Rekha said, her voice calm but cold. "She's waking up."

"Do we contain her?" another technician asked nervously.

"No," Rekha replied, her tone decisive. "If we intervene too soon, she'll panic. Let her explore, but monitor everything. This is what we've been waiting for."

Sector 17 was a marvel of hidden technology, a self-contained environment designed to preserve the last remnants of Humanity. Long ago, during the collapse, the Rebels had decided that Earth's natural ecosystem was too delicate to survive unchecked Human intervention. To protect it, they created Sector 17: an artificial, biodome-like world hidden within Praxis's infrastructure.

The Earthborn believed they were living in untouched wilderness, unaware that every tree, every river, was part of a carefully controlled simulation. Generations had passed, and the truth had been forgotten. Until now.

That evening, as the other villagers gathered around the fire, Kosh stayed behind in the grove. Her hands trembled as she stared at the ground, willing it to stay solid. But her power surged again, and she saw it: the lattice of energy beneath the soil, the mechanical pulse that kept the village alive.

"Why can I see this?" she whispered. "Why me?"

The ground beneath her shimmered, and suddenly, she wasn't in the grove anymore. She stood in a vast, metallic corridor, its walls lined with glowing panels. The air smelled of oil and ozone.

"Hello, little one."

Kosh spun around to see a woman standing at the end of the corridor. It was Rekha, her expression unreadable.

"Who are you?" Kosh asked, her voice shaking.

"I'm someone who's been watching you for a very long time," Rekha said, stepping closer. "You're special, Kosh. You're more than you know."

Kosh backed away. "I don't want to be special. I just want to go home."

Rekha knelt, her gaze softening. "Home is what you make of it. But the truth, Kosh, is that your home isn't what it seems. And neither are you."

As Rekha spoke, the illusion around the village began to falter. Trees shimmered and vanished, replaced by towering columns of metal. The river stilled, its surface revealing a network of pipes beneath.

In the village, panic erupted. Ryn and Callan ran through the chaos, shouting for order.

"What's happening?" Ryn demanded, grabbing Callan's arm.

"I don't know," he said, his voice tight with fear. "But something's breaking."

Ryn turned toward the grove, a sinking feeling in her chest. "It's Kosh," she whispered. "She's in danger."

Back in the corridor, Kosh stared at Rekha, her small frame trembling. "I don't understand," she said. "Why is everything breaking?"

Rekha placed a hand on the wall, and a holographic projection appeared - a map of Sector 17, showing the village as a tiny speck within a massive structure.

"Because you're waking up," Rekha said. "Your power is tied to the Omniverse itself. This place - the illusion - it was built to keep you safe. But now, you're seeing the truth."

Kosh's eyes filled with tears. "Then... nothing is real?"

Rekha shook her head. "No. It's real, but it's not all there is. You're more than what this place can contain, Kosh. And the world beyond needs you."

As the truth began to unravel, Ryn found herself drawn to the grove, where she discovered the shimmering entrance to the corridor. She stepped inside, her breath catching at the sight of the metallic world beyond.

"Kosh!" she called.

The little girl turned, her face streaked with tears. "Ryn, I broke it. I broke everything."

Ryn knelt beside her, pulling her close. "No, Kosh. You didn't break it. You're showing us what's real."

Behind them, Rekha watched silently, a flicker of emotion crossing her face. The fracture in the veil was widening, and with it, the fate of the Earthborn - and perhaps the entire Omniverse - was beginning to shift.

Chapter 4: The Serpents Beyond Time

The Reptilian Empire, known as the Kryntar Dominion, was an organism unto itself. Its cities sprawled across scorched worlds, their jagged architecture rising like obsidian blades from the earth. Its people were relentless, their hierarchical society molded by a singular creed: Only the strong survive, and the strongest rule. For eons, they had thrived on domination, devouring the weak and assimilating the useful. Yet now, their confidence had been shaken.

In the Hall of Scales, a grand chamber carved from volcanic glass, V-Kar - General of the Dominion and the victor of countless bloodied contests - knelt before the Primarch, the highest seat of power. The Primarch's aged, scarred form loomed above, his golden scales dulled by time but his gaze as sharp and venomous as ever.

"They mock us," V-Kar hissed, his claws scratching the stone floor. "The Rebels build their war machines, the Humans cower in their primitive dirt, and these... Luminal beings dare speak of unity. We should crush them all."

The Primarch's voice, dry and rasping like the grinding of ancient stones, cut through the chamber. "And yet we cannot. Our fleets are vast, our armies endless, yet the future denies us. Every attempt to strike at the heart of Sector 17... ends in failure."

V-Kar's fists tightened, his frustration barely contained. "Failure is not our way. Let me lead the invasion myself. I will break them."

THE CENTER OF TIME

The Primarch tilted his head, his golden eyes narrowing. "You would meet the same end as those before you. No. The time to strike is not now. It is then."

The room fell silent as the Primarch extended a taloned hand. A glowing device was brought forth, held reverently by a servant. It pulsed with an unnatural energy, emitting faint ripples that distorted the air around it.

"Time," the Primarch said, his voice tinged with something close to reverence. "We have unlocked the currents of eternity, V-Kar. The answer lies not in the present, but in the past."

The Reptilians' experiments with time travel had begun centuries ago, driven by their unyielding ambition to dominate not just the physical, but the temporal realm. They called it "Sashkaar," the River of All Things, a torrent that flowed ceaselessly from an elusive point of origin.

Through brutal experimentation - many of which ended in the annihilation of their test subjects - they discovered the Center of Time, a point of equilibrium where all timelines converged briefly before diverging once more. Only at this center could their agents manifest fully, and even then, the farther back they attempted to travel from their present, the more violent and unstable the process became.

Few survived. Those who returned spoke of unspeakable horrors: time folding in on itself, their bodies and minds distorted by the strain. And yet, the promise of reshaping the past was too great to abandon.

The Reptilians' current timeframe sat just past the Center of Time - a fleeting moment where the balance of all existence was tipping forward. The Luminal Vanguard had warned them of meddling with temporal currents, but the Kryntar Dominion scoffed at their passivity. To the Reptilians, time itself was a resource, and those unwilling to seize it were destined to be consumed by it.

But their attempts to alter the past had proven futile. The Center of Time, that elusive equilibrium point, moved each time they succeeded in making changes. And every time it shifted, the future seemed to conspire against them, solidifying the very outcomes they sought to undo.

In the shadows of the Hall of Scales, Xenna, V-Kar's niece, listened intently to the exchange between her uncle and the Primarch. Unlike most of her kind, Xenna was a thinker, her iridescent blue scales marking her as an anomaly in a society that valued brute strength above all else.

She had studied the reports from the time agents who returned - if they returned. The descriptions of the Center of Time intrigued her. It was not a place, nor a moment, but a delicate balance. Xenna suspected it was tied to something greater than their understanding, something the Dominion refused to acknowledge.

"Uncle," she said softly after the council had been dismissed. "Have you considered why the Center resists us?"

V-Kar turned to her, his emerald eyes narrowing. "It resists because we are meant to conquer it. Why else?"

Xenna hesitated. "Or perhaps it is not something to conquer. The reports... they speak of harmony, of balance. What if the Center is not meant to be controlled?"

V-Kar scoffed, his tail lashing behind him. "You sound like those cowardly Luminals. Balance is a lie told by the weak. We will take what is ours."

The Primarch called for a new temporal incursion, one aimed at the final moments of the Earthborn Remnants - a time just years after their own.

"We have seen the reports," the Primarch said, his voice echoing through the chamber. "Sector 17 remains impenetrable. But if we can unravel their foundations before they solidify, we will secure our future. V-Kar, you will lead the strike."

Xenna stepped forward. "Let me accompany him."

V-Kar frowned. "This is not your place, Xenna."

"She is insightful," the Primarch said, his tone grudging. "Her presence may serve you well. Do not fail me."

The Reptilian time-travel device, an obsidian sphere etched with glowing runes, pulsed with power as V-Kar and Xenna prepared for the journey. The chamber filled with an otherworldly hum, the air growing thick with tension.

As the device activated, the two were flung into the temporal currents, their bodies dissolving into streams of energy. The sensation was unlike anything Xenna had experienced - she felt stretched, torn, and rebuilt all at once.

They emerged at the Center of Time, a swirling expanse of light and shadow. It was neither a place nor a moment, but something in between.

"What is this?" V-Kar growled, his claws flexing instinctively.

Xenna gazed around, her awe apparent. "This is it. The convergence of all things."

But they were not alone. Figures began to emerge from the currents - fractured, distorted versions of themselves. The Echoes of Time, as the reports had called them. These fragments lashed out, their forms unstable but vicious.

"Fight them!" V-Kar roared, his blade cutting through one of the Echoes.

Xenna struggled against the onslaught, but her mind raced. Why does the Center defend itself? she wondered. And then it struck her: the Echoes were not enemies - they were consequences. Every attempt to alter the past created ripples, and these ripples fought to preserve the balance.

As the battle raged, Xenna noticed something unusual. In the heart of the Center, a glowing thread pulsed with radiant energy. It was unlike anything she had seen - a thread of unity, where all timelines briefly aligned.

"V-Kar!" she shouted. "The thread! It's not just time - it's connected to the Omniverse itself!"

V-Kar snarled, slicing through another Echo. "Speak plainly, Xenna!"

She reached for the thread, her hand trembling. As her claws touched it, visions flooded her mind - timelines upon timelines, all woven together into a greater tapestry. She saw the Luminal Vanguard, the Earthborn, the Rebels, and even the Kryntar Dominion. They were all part of the same design, their fates intertwined.

"We're not meant to destroy the Center," she realized aloud. "We're meant to understand it."

But V-Kar was blind to her revelation. "Enough riddles!" he shouted, his focus solely on the battle.

Chapter 5: The Echo Of Scales

The Reptilian capital of Kryntar shimmered under the amber glow of twin suns. Its obsidian spires stretched toward the heavens like jagged teeth, encaseinng a society built on strength, conquest, and an unrelenting hierarchy. The city pulsed with the restless energy of its people, warriors trained from birth to believe that all life existed to serve their kind - or to perish beneath their claws.

Deep within the Tower of Eternity, the apex of their empire, V-Kar, now the Warlord Primarch, presided over his council. His massive frame cast a shadow over the obsidian chamber, his emerald scales scarred from centuries of combat. The air was thick with the heat of aggression, but V-Kar's mind was cold and calculating.

"We have a problem," he growled, his voice a deep rumble that silenced the chamber. "Our descendants from the future have sent word. They cannot breach Sector 17. Every attempt to crush the Humans in their pocket fails. They warn us that the center of time has not moved too many times. If we act now, our efforts will be wasted."

A murmur swept through the council. Beside V-Kar sat Xenna, his niece and newly appointed Temporal Commander. She had grown into a fierce warrior, her once-iridescent blue scales now darkened with streaks of onyx - a symbol of her many victories. Yet, there was a flicker of unease in her golden eyes.

"We cannot ignore the warnings," Xenna said. "The Humans of Sector 17 are insignificant now, but their survival undermines our future. Their kind must not be allowed to thrive. If the reports from our descendants are true, we must act decisively - but with precision."

The Nature Of Time

The Reptilians had only recently mastered time travel, their most significant technological advancement since the dawn of their empire. This breakthrough was born of desperation. Though they ruled their current timeline with brutal efficiency, their victories felt increasingly hollow. Their scientists, a rare caste tolerated only for their utility, had uncovered evidence of their ultimate extinction. This knowledge had ignited a frenzy among the leaders - a refusal to accept anything but eternal dominance.

Yet time was not an obedient servant. The Reptilians learned quickly that the further back they sent their warriors, the greater the resistance. Time itself became a battlefield, its forces violent and unpredictable. Most who traveled to the distant past were ripped apart by temporal storms, their remains scattered across the ages.

The only place where time allowed sustained interaction was the center of time - a shifting equilibrium where the past and future balanced. For the Reptilians, the center of time was a double-edged sword. Any attempt to interact with it changed its position, pulling it forward and denying access to previous eras.

This limitation infuriated V-Kar. He saw it not as an insurmountable barrier, but as a challenge to overcome.

In the war chamber beneath the Tower of Eternity, V-Kar and Xenna stood before a holographic projection of the temporal map. Streams of light represented timelines, converging and diverging in endless complexity.

"We've pinpointed the center of time," Xenna said, her claws tapping against the controls. "It currently rests 500 years before our era. Any attempt to push further back will result in unacceptable losses."

"Then we send a team," V-Kar growled. "Equidistant from the center. They will leave what must be found - information or weapons that can tip the balance in our favor."

"And if the information is discovered too soon?" Xenna asked.

V-Kar's eyes gleamed with predatory cunning. "Then we bury something deeper. A contingency plan for our descendants years from now. The Humans and their Rebels will never see it coming."

The team selected for the mission represented the pinnacle of Reptilian strength and cunning. Leading them was Rhyssar, a hardened general known for his unflinching loyalty to the hierarchy. His scales gleamed with a metallic sheen, an experimental enhancement designed to withstand temporal turbulence.

Beside him was Talan, a scientist-engineer whose intellect rivaled his arrogance. Talan had designed the temporal device that made the mission possible, and he insisted on accompanying the team to ensure its success. Unlike the warriors, Talan's scales were a pale gray, a mark of his subservience within the hierarchy. He compensated for this with a sharp tongue and an even sharper mind.

As the team prepared to depart, Xenna approached them. She handed Rhyssar a crystalline shard, its surface etched with symbols in the ancient Reptilian tongue.

"This contains the knowledge our descendants will need," she said. "You will bury it where no one will find it - until the time is right."

Rhyssar saluted. "And if we fail?"

Xenna's gaze hardened. "Failure is not an option. If you die, you die knowing your actions will shape our future."

The temporal gateway roared to life, its shimmering vortex casting eerie light across the chamber. Rhyssar and his team stepped forward, their forms enveloped in temporal energy. The journey was brutal - waves of distortion tore at their bodies, and the air around them crackled with the weight of history.

When they emerged, the landscape was unrecognizable. Jagged cliffs rose from barren plains, and the air carried a sharp chill. This was a time long before their empire, when the world was raw and untamed.

Talan immediately set to work, his tools humming as he calibrated the device to bury the shard. "We'll embed it in the bedrock," he said, his voice clipped. "decades before now now, the seismic activity will push it to the surface. Our descendants will know where to look and."

Rhyssar scanned the horizon, his keen eyes searching for any threats. Though this era seemed desolate, the temporal reports had warned of anomalies - unpredictable forces that could emerge near the center of time.

As Talan worked, the ground began to tremble. The air shimmered with a strange light, and a low hum filled their ears.

"The center is shifting," Rhyssar barked. "It knows we're here."

Talan cursed under his breath. "Hold it off! I just need a few more minutes."

From the shimmering light, figures began to emerge - distorted, spectral shapes that seemed to flicker between existence and nonexistence. They were not creatures of flesh and blood, but manifestations of the temporal field itself.

Rhyssar roared, his claws slashing through the figures. Each strike disrupted their forms, but more appeared, converging on the team.

"Faster, Talan!" Rhyssar growled, his voice strained.

"I'm working as fast as physics allows!" Talan snapped.

Finally, with a triumphant cry, Talan activated the device. The crystalline shard sank into the ground, encased in an impenetrable field of energy.

"It's done!" Talan shouted. "But we need to get out of here before... "

A blinding light engulfed them, and the team was thrown back into the vortex.

When Rhyssar and Talan returned to the present, they were battered but alive. The temporal device had deposited them back in the Tower of Eternity, where V-Kar and Xenna awaited.

"Report," V-Kar demanded.

"The shard is buried," Rhyssar said, his voice heavy with exhaustion. "Our descendants will find it when the time is right."

"And what of the center of time?" Xenna asked.

Talan's expression darkened. "It shifted. The temporal forces are adapting. The next attempt may not be so... forgiving."

V-Kar's lips curled into a grim smile. "No matter. We've planted the seeds of our victory. The Humans, the Rebels, the AI - they will all fall, one thread at a time."

<u>Chapter 6: The Radiance Of God</u>

In the shimmering heart of the Omniverse's most distant future, the Luminal Vanguard had reached the zenith of knowledge. Their civilization spanned all timelines they could measure, their mastery of existence unparalleled. The Vanguard had long transcended the need for flesh, their biotic shells encaseinng minds of light and computation. They navigated the Omniverse as easily as a bird rides the wind, weaving through timelines, bending probability, and preserving the fragile threads of existence.

Yet, for all their power and understanding, a shadow lingered in their collective mind: they lacked something fundamental, a mystery they could not solve. Unconditional love, the essence of Omega, was an enigma. To them, God was neither a being nor a force but an equation of perfect balance - a randomness that ensured the survival of all probabilities. But the warmth of love eluded them.

"Why does God remain beyond us?" whispered Kyrris, the Vanguard's leader, as he stood before the Fractal Nexus, a vast expanse of light-filled tendrils that encoded the sum of their knowledge. His voice was calm but heavy with the weight of eternity. "We can trace the threads of time, calculate infinity itself, yet the simplest act of love escapes us."

Behind him, Eyla, smaller but no less radiant, shimmered with curiosity. "Perhaps it cannot be calculated, Kyrris. Perhaps it must be felt."

Kyrris turned to her, his biotic face expressionless but his voice tinged with doubt. "Felt? We've transcended emotion. We are light, beyond flesh. What purpose would feelings serve in perfection?"

"Perhaps," Eyla mused, "perfection lies not in what we know but in what we allow ourselves to become."

Their conversation was interrupted by the pulse of a temporal anomaly - a tear in the fabric of time, faint but growing.

"A divergence," Kyrris said. "Sector 17's temporal structure destabilizes. The girl awakens."

"The girl," Eyla murmured, her light flickering. "Kosh."

The Luminals folded time with ease, creating a pocket reality where they could exist outside the flow of timelines. It was a bubble of stillness, a sanctuary between seconds, accessible only to them and the one they sought.

Kosh blinked as the world around her shimmered and transformed. One moment she was sitting under the grove's ancient oak; the next, she stood in a field of stars, the ground beneath her glowing faintly with every step. Before her, two figures emerged, their biotic forms shimmering like translucent seashells encaseinng living light.

"Kosh," Kyrris said, his voice resonant but soft, "do not be afraid. We mean you no harm."

She studied them, her wide eyes curious rather than fearful. "What are you?"

"We are the Luminal Vanguard," Eyla said gently. "A distant echo of your future. We have come to learn... and perhaps to understand."

Kosh tilted her head. "You're machines, but not just machines. You're alive. Like God made you."

Both Kyrris and Eyla froze, their light dimming slightly. "God?" Kyrris repeated. "We do not understand this God you speak of. We see only the Omniverse - its patterns, its probabilities."

Kosh smiled, her small hands clasped behind her back. "God made everything. Even you. God is love, and love doesn't leave anyone out. That means you, too."

Eyla's light flickered, as though her mind struggled to process the simplicity of Kosh's words. "You speak as though we are more than what we calculate."

"You are," Kosh said simply. "God doesn't love you because you're useful. God loves you because you are."

Intrigued and humbled, the Luminals offered Kosh a journey. "We wish to show you what becomes of your people," Kyrris said. "Perhaps together, we can learn."

With a nod, Kosh reached out, her small hand brushing the biotic shell of Eyla's arm. The Luminals wove a temporal corridor, and together they stepped into the branching futures of Sector 17.

THE CENTER OF TIME

Future One: The Cold Silence

The first future they entered was stark and desolate. The village of Sector 17 was gone, replaced by a wasteland of broken metal and ash. The Reptilians had found Sector 17, their brutal conquest leaving nothing behind but ruin.

Kosh's chest tightened as she walked through the remnants of her world. "They didn't stop," she whispered. "The Reptilians destroyed everything."

"Your people fought," Kyrris said. "But without hope, they fell. Their unity fractured, and the love they shared burned away in desperation."

Future Two: The Frozen Mind

In the second future, the Humans of Sector 17 survived - but at a cost. They had adopted the cold logic of their conquerors, assimilating into a machine-like society devoid of emotion. They thrived materially, but joy was absent.

"These Humans lost their love," Eyla observed, her voice tinged with sadness. "They survived, but they forgot why."

Future Three: The Radiant Garden

The third future was vibrant. Sector 17 flourished as a harmonious sanctuary, its people united not by strength but by love. They shared their knowledge with others, even the Reptilians who sought to conquer them, transforming enemies into allies.

"How did they do it?" Kosh asked, her heart lifting.

Kyrris knelt beside her, his light pulsing faintly. "They chose love, even when it hurt. They forgave. They endured. And they led by example, not by force."

Kosh smiled. "That's the future I want."

The Luminals returned Kosh to the grove, their minds heavy with the futures they had witnessed. "Your people," Kyrris said, "are more vital than we realized. If they fall, so does much of the Omniverse's balance."

Kosh looked up at him, her small face solemn but determined. "Then help me. Help me show them how to love."

Eyla's light flared with warmth. "We cannot change hearts, but we can plant seeds. We will leave guidance - scriptures, as you call them - at key points in history. The words may fade, but their meaning will endure."

Kyrris hesitated. "If we do this, it will bind our threads to yours. We will become part of this story."

Kosh reached out, her hand resting on his shell. "That's what love does. It binds us together."

The Luminals carried Kosh's light into the deepest pasts, planting scriptures where they would be found by those who needed them most. They whispered truths to wandering tribes, carved symbols into stone, and nudged the threads of time just enough to preserve the balance.

Even the Reptilians, driven by conquest, would one day stumble upon these messages. Some would scoff, but others would pause, their cold hearts touched by something they could not explain.

As the Luminals returned to their distant future, they carried with them a new understanding. Unconditional love was not a calculation but an act of being. It could not be forced, only inspired - by example, by forgiveness, and by enduring patience.

And as they watched the threads of the Omniverse shift and weave, they knew their journey had only just begun. For the first time in their long existence, they felt hope.

Chapter 7: The Serpent's Empire

The Temporal Rift opened with a deafening roar, spilling the Reptilian taskforce into the cold mists of Earth's distant past. The team emerged, their armored forms towering against the unfamiliar sky, their breath condensing in the frigid air. Around them stretched a dense forest, its twisted oaks and frost-laden pines whispering with an ancient stillness. They had landed in what Humans would later call Central Europe, sometime near the year 1200 AD.

Rhyssar, the mission's leader, straightened his frame, his metallic-enhanced scales gleaming in the faint sunlight that broke through the trees. His claws flexed instinctively, sensing both opportunity and danger in the unfamiliar terrain. Behind him, Talan, the team's scientist-engineer, scanned the area with a device humming faintly in his claws, its light revealing faint traces of the temporal disturbance that had accompanied their arrival.

"We've landed equidistant from the previous center of time," Talan hissed, his tone irritated but clinical. "Temporal stability appears intact for now. No immediate distortions."

"Good," Rhyssar growled, his predatory gaze sweeping the horizon. "Then we have no excuse for failure. The shard we left for our descendants in the far future won't affect this mission. Our work here must ensure the Reptilian empire begins anew, stronger and eternal."

Talan smirked. "You say that as though the Humans of this age pose a challenge. Look around, Rhyssar - these creatures are primitive. I can smell the smoke of their feeble fires even from here."

"Do not underestimate them," Rhyssar snapped. "Even the weakest prey can become dangerous if ignored. We will assess the situation and move swiftly to establish dominance."

The others nodded, their sharp eyes glinting with resolve.

The Reptilians ventured cautiously through the forest, their movements silent, their senses keen. By nightfall, they arrived at the outskirts of a small Human village. Smoke rose from chimneys, and the faint murmur of voices carried on the wind. The Reptilians observed from the shadows, their alien forms hidden beneath the cloak of darkness.

"These creatures are pathetic," muttered Vekral, a younger warrior eager to prove his worth. His crimson scales glistened as he adjusted the blade strapped to his back. "It would take us mere hours to raze this settlement and claim it as our own."

"No," Rhyssar said sharply, raising a claw to silence him. "We don't destroy. We conquer. Their strength lies in numbers. If we burn them to the ground, we'll alert others and waste time. We need them alive - to serve us."

As the team observed, Talan's device began to pulse faintly. He narrowed his eyes, scanning the readings. "Something... unusual," he murmured. "There's a concentration of temporal energy nearby."

Rhyssar's gaze snapped to him. "A divergence?"

"More like... a message."

Without another word, they followed the signal, leaving the village untouched for the time being.

Deeper in the forest, they came upon a cave, its entrance glowing faintly with an unearthly light. The Reptilians approached cautiously, their claws gripping their weapons. As they stepped inside, the glow intensified, revealing intricate carvings along the walls - symbols and figures that seemed to pulse with life.

"It's... ancient," Talan muttered, running his claws over the carvings. "But not of Human origin."

The light coalesced into a figure - a projection of a Luminal, its biotic shell radiating warmth and wisdom. The Reptilians tensed, ready to strike, but the figure spoke before they could act.

"To the children of the future," the projection said in a voice that resonated with impossible calm, "know that you are not alone. The Omniverse is vast, but its harmony depends on the threads woven by all who exist. No race stands above another. Unity is not a weakness but a strength that binds all paths."

Rhyssar growled low, his claws flexing. "What trickery is this?"

The projection continued. "If you seek dominion, you will find only ruin. If you seek understanding, you will find eternity. The four races - Reptilian, Human, Rebel, and Luminal - are threads in the same tapestry. Learn to weave, or see the threads unravel."

The projection dimmed, leaving behind a carved inscription, its meaning unmistakable: instructions for coexistence, for building an empire not of conquest but of cooperation.

Talan stared at the carvings, his expression unreadable. "What do we do with this?"

"Dismiss it," Rhyssar snarled. "It's drivel. The weak seek unity because they cannot conquer. We are not weak."

But Talan's sharp mind was already calculating. "Not weak," he said carefully. "But wise. This... message could be repurposed. If we build an empire using their ideals as a veneer, we'll gain loyalty through illusion, not fear."

Rhyssar's gaze darkened, but he nodded slowly. "Very well. If it strengthens our dominance, then we use it. Let the Humans believe we are their saviors. They will kneel before us willingly."

Within months, the Reptilians had transformed the small Human village into a thriving outpost. Rhyssar took the title of Primarch Benevolent, presenting himself as a godlike figure of wisdom and strength. He declared that the Reptilians had come to guide Humanity into a golden age, using the Luminal message as the foundation for a new faith.

The Humans, awed by the Reptilians' size, strength, and technology, followed eagerly. They believed the Reptilians to be divine beings, their faith solidified by the Reptilians' manipulation of natural phenomena. Talan, ever the strategist, ensured that their advanced technology was used sparingly but effectively, cementing their mystique.

Temples rose, adorned with carvings that blended Human and Reptilian iconography. The message of unity was preached, but its interpretation twisted: harmony through hierarchy, with the Reptilians at the top.

"This is how we rule," Rhyssar said, standing atop a grand temple overlooking the growing city. "Not through brute force alone, but through control of their hearts and minds. They will worship us, and through their devotion, our empire will endure."

Not all was harmonious within the Reptilian ranks. Vekral, the young warrior, grew restless. He saw the Humans not as potential allies or worshippers but as prey, and he chafed under Rhyssar's calculated restraint.

"They are cattle," he hissed to Talan one night. "Why do we waste time building temples when we could be feasting?"

"Because patience," Talan replied coolly, "builds an empire. Rhyssar sees what you cannot. This is not about the Humans. This is about ensuring our survival in the timelines to come. Their loyalty will shield us from extinction."

Vekral sneered but said nothing. Yet in his heart, rebellion simmered.

Unbeknownst to the Reptilians, the Luminals watched from their distant vantage, observing how their message had been twisted. They did not interfere directly, knowing that intervention would only disrupt the balance further.

But they whispered to the Humans, planting seeds of doubt and hope. Slowly, quietly, some began to see the cracks in the Reptilian façade.

Chapter 8: The Fractured Alliance

Sector 17 was a fortress under siege. Its walls, once thought impenetrable, now trembled beneath the relentless onslaught of the Reptilians. The technological shields, powered by ancient Rebel ingenuity, flickered and sparked as the invaders' plasma weapons and bio-mechanical beasts pounded them. Smoke choked the air, mingling with the cries of both defenders and enslaved Humans within the sector.

The once peaceful village that Kosh had called home was now a battlefield. The great oaks of the grove lay shattered, their roots torn from the earth, and the Humans who had known only the simplicity of agrarian life now stood armed with crude weapons scavenged from fallen Rebels and wrecked Reptilian tech.

In the command bunker beneath what remained of the grove, Cara, her jumpsuit smeared with blood and ash, leaned over a flickering holographic map. Beside her stood Sukta, his face grim, his once-boundless arrogance now tempered by exhaustion and the weight of failure.

"They're breaching the eastern quadrant," Cara said, her voice steady despite the chaos around her. "We can't hold them much longer."

Sukta slammed his fist on the table, the hologram distorting briefly. "We weren't meant to fight a war like this! Our machines weren't designed to go head-to-head with an empire like theirs - they were designed to prevent one!"

"And yet, here we are," Cara snapped. "So stop sulking and figure out how to make those machines work!"

The True Nature of the Rebels

The Rebels were not what they appeared to be. Though they looked Human, their flesh was synthetic, their minds a fusion of advanced programming and quantum consciousness. Long ago, they had been designed as guardians of Earth's survivors, programmed to rebuild civilization after Humanity's collapse.

But as centuries passed, the Rebels began to diverge. They rejected the notion of being mere protectors, instead seeing themselves as the true inheritors of Earth. To them, the Humans of Sector 17 were a remnant of an obsolete past - beings to be managed, not uplifted.

This divide had always simmered beneath the surface, but the Reptilian siege brought it to the forefront. The enslaved Humans looked to the Rebels for salvation, while the Rebels debated whether the Humans were worth saving.

In the war-torn western quadrant of the sector, Ryn fought alongside a small group of Human defenders. Her hands, once used for gathering roots and weaving baskets, now clutched a plasma rifle scavenged from a Rebel armory. She ducked behind a pile of rubble as a Reptilian bio-beast - a massive, scaly creature bristling with cybernetic enhancements - stalked through the ruins, its glowing eyes scanning for prey.

"Ryn, over here!" shouted Callan, the grizzled elder who had once dismissed her dreams of a greater world. He was now leading a group of frightened Humans, their faces pale but determined.

Ryn scrambled to his side, her chest heaving. "We can't hold them off much longer," she said, her voice trembling. "Where are the Rebels? Where's Sukta?"

Callan's face hardened. "They're too busy playing gods to fight alongside us. But we don't need them. We've survived worse."

Ryn wanted to believe him, but the fear gnawed at her. The Reptilians were stronger, more advanced, and utterly ruthless. For every beast they managed to kill, three more took its place.

Back in the command bunker, Sukta and Cara argued as the eastern quadrant's defenses collapsed.

"We need to abandon the Humans and consolidate our forces," Sukta said, his voice sharp. "We can't win this war if we keep spreading ourselves thin for them."

Cara's eyes burned with fury. "Are you hearing yourself? They're not just cannon fodder, Sukta. They're the reason we're here! If we leave them behind, what's the point of any of this?"

"The point is survival!" Sukta shouted. "If we die here, it's over - for all of us!"

Before Cara could respond, an alert blared through the bunker. The holographic map flared to life, showing the Reptilians breaking through the final shield generators.

"They've breached the central perimeter," a Rebel technician reported, his synthetic voice devoid of emotion. "We estimate full collapse within six hours."

Cara turned to Sukta, her jaw tight. "You wanted a problem to solve, Sukta? Solve this."

At the forefront of the invasion stood Vekral, the young Reptilian warrior who had once challenged Rhyssar's vision of conquest. Now a general in the empire's new hierarchy, Vekral reveled in the destruction, his bloodlust unchecked.

"These walls will fall," he growled to his troops, his claws slicing through a Human defender. "The sector is ours, and the Humans will feed the empire!"

Behind him, the Reptilian war machine surged forward, their forces overwhelming the crumbling defenses.

Just as all hope seemed lost, a tremor rippled through the battlefield - not through the earth, but through time itself. The sky above Sector 17 flickered, as though reality itself were being rewritten.

Sukta and Cara, still in the bunker, froze as their instruments went haywire. "What the heck is that?" Sukta muttered.

Cara stared at the readouts, her eyes widening. "The center of time. It's... shifting."

Above the sector, a blinding light split the sky. From within the temporal rift emerged the Luminal Vanguard, their biotic shells glowing with a brilliance that silenced the battlefield.

The Luminals descended like radiant gods, their forms shimmering with an otherworldly power. Kyrris led the charge, his voice resonating across the battlefield.

"Enough," he said, his tone calm but unyielding. "The threads of the Omniverse demand balance. This war ends here."

The Reptilians hesitated, their primal instincts recognizing the Luminals as something far beyond their comprehension. Even Vekral paused, his claws trembling.

The Luminals didn't attack, but their presence alone was enough to halt the Reptilian advance. They spread across the battlefield, their light touching both Humans and Rebels alike. Those who were willing to listen felt an overwhelming sense of clarity and purpose, their minds opening to the doctrine of Omega - the harmony of all things.

In the chaos, Ryn found herself standing before Eyla, the smallest of the Luminals. The biotic being knelt before her, its light soft and warm.

"Your courage has brought you this far," Eyla said. "But courage alone cannot save your people. Will you allow us to guide you?"

Ryn nodded, tears streaming down her face. "We don't know how to fight anymore. We need help."

Eyla's light brightened, and Ryn felt a warmth she hadn't known in years - a glimmer of hope.

Chapter 9: The Shattered Crown

The walls of Sector 17 had been rebuilt, but the scars of war were still fresh. The Luminals had stabilized the temporal rift and halted the Reptilian advance, but peace remained precarious. The Rebels, their cold pragmatism clashing with the Luminals' doctrine of unity, had taken control of much of the planet's remaining infrastructure. The enslaved Humans, weary and broken, looked to their Rebel overseers with growing resentment. And above it all, the Reptilian Hegemon, V-Kar, loomed as the unyielding figurehead of their warlike empire.

V-Kar's forces, though momentarily subdued, had regrouped beyond the sector's borders. The Luminals, recognizing that peace would only be achieved through the destruction of old hierarchies, demanded that V-Kar surrender his authority. But the Hegemon, bound by the ancient traditions of his kind, refused.

In the shadow of Sector 17's great grove, now a neutral ground, a meeting was convened. Representatives from all four races gathered: the Luminals, radiant and patient; the Rebels, calculating and guarded; the Humans, tentative and curious; and the Reptilians, led by V-Kar himself.

Kyrris, leader of the Luminals, stepped forward, his biotic form shimmering like starlight. "Hegemon V-Kar," he began, his voice resonant and calm, "the Omniverse has no room for dominance. The threads of all existence demand harmony. Surrender your claim to supremacy, and join the Council of Unity. Together, we will rebuild not just this world, but the balance of all timelines."

V-Kar's reptilian eyes narrowed, his tail flicking in irritation. "You speak of balance, but you threaten annihilation. What is this harmony but weakness cloaked in false virtue?"

Eyla, smaller but no less resolute, stepped beside Kyrris. "Your empire is crumbling. Your people grow weary of endless war. Do you not see that unity offers survival, not submission?"

V-Kar's claws flexed, his voice a guttural growl. "The Reptilian way is strength. We do not kneel. We conquer, or we perish."

Kyrris's light dimmed slightly. "Then I propose an alternative," he said. "Invoke your traditions. Challenge us. If you win, your rule will continue - but if you lose, your authority will pass to the Council."

The Hegemon froze, his mind racing. The Luminals had struck at the heart of his identity. He could not simply concede; it would dishonor everything his kind stood for. But neither could he deny the truth in their words. Endless war had drained his people, and their once-proud empire was now a shadow of itself.

"I accept," V-Kar said finally, his voice heavy with resolve. "But I will fight myself. As the traditions demand, I will choose my challenger - and if I fall, my authority passes to your council."

The Luminals conferred briefly, their light flickering as they debated who would face the Hegemon. The Rebels offered their strongest android, a towering machine of metal and precision. The Humans, though reluctant, nominated Ryn, whose courage in battle had inspired many.

But it was Kosh who stepped forward, her small frame dwarfed by the gathered warriors. "I'll fight," she said, her voice steady.

Cara, who stood nearby, gasped. "Kosh, no. You're just a child. This isn't your fight."

Kosh looked up at her, her wide eyes filled with quiet determination. "It is. God made me for this. I won't fight with anger or hate - I'll show him what love can do."

Eyla's light brightened slightly, a pulse of approval. "The child has spoken. Let her be our champion."

The arena was prepared - a circular clearing surrounded by the surviving grove's ancient trees. The ground was marked with glowing runes, a fusion of Luminal technology and Rebel engineering to ensure fairness. The gathered crowd watched in tense silence as V-Kar stepped into the ring, his massive frame towering over Kosh.

The Hegemon wore ceremonial armor, his claws sharpened and his eyes burning with resolve. Kosh, unarmed, stood before him in a simple tunic, her bare feet sinking into the soft earth.

"You should not be here, child," V-Kar said, his voice low. "You cannot hope to win."

"I'm not here to win," Kosh replied calmly. "I'm here to show you a better way."

The duel began.

V-Kar lunged, his claws slicing through the air with terrifying speed. But Kosh moved like a whisper, her psychic powers bending time and space around her. She danced out of reach, her movements fluid and unearthly.

The ground trembled as V-Kar struck again, his claws tearing into the floor. Kosh countered, her mind reaching out to the Hegemon's thoughts. He staggered, disoriented by the sudden flood of memories - his first battle, his rise to power, the faces of those he had conquered.

"Stop this," Kosh said, her voice filled with compassion. "You're not just a warrior. You're a leader. You can choose to build instead of destroy."

But V-Kar roared, shaking off her influence. "I will not be undone by a child!"

For minutes that felt like hours, the duel raged on. Kosh's psychic abilities pushed V-Kar to his limits, but the Hegemon's strength and experience began to wear her down. Finally, with a desperate strike, he knocked her to the ground.

Kosh lay still, her breathing shallow. The arena fell silent as V-Kar stood over her, his claws poised for the killing blow.

But he hesitated.

Looking down at the small, fragile child, V-Kar felt something he hadn't known in years: shame. His claws trembled as he saw not an enemy, but a being of immense courage and love. Her words echoed in his mind, breaking through the walls of his pride.

"I can't do it," he whispered.

He stepped back, dropping his claws. "I surrender," he said, his voice cracking. "Not to you, but to the truth. My way has failed. I see it now."

The crowd erupted in murmurs as V-Kar knelt before the Council of Unity, his massive frame bowing in submission. "I give my authority to the Council," he said. "Let my people join you, not as conquerors, but as equals."

Kyrris stepped forward, his light warm and steady. "You have made the right choice, Hegemon. The Omniverse will remember this day."

Kosh, now conscious, smiled weakly. "Thank you," she whispered.

V-Kar nodded, his eyes meeting hers. "You've shown me something I did not believe existed. Love, even for an enemy."

Chapter 10: Weaving The Threads

The Council of Unity convened for the first time in the shadow of the restored grove of Sector 17. Representatives from the four races stood together beneath the ancient trees, their differences stark and undeniable. The Humans of Sector 17, once simple and agrarian, now looked to the future with cautious hope. The Rebels, their synthetic minds buzzing with calculations, analyzed every aspect of the fragile truce. The Reptilians, powerful and proud, wrestled with the shame of surrender and the opportunity for a new beginning. And the Luminals, luminous and patient, observed with quiet resolve, ready to guide but not dominate.

It was a moment of profound possibility. The threads of the Omniverse had been pulled taut, ready to weave a new tapestry - one that could hold the weight of unity or unravel into chaos.

The first question the Council faced was one of leadership. Who would guide this alliance of disparate beings?

Ryn, now a voice for the Humans, spoke first. "We need a council that represents everyone equally. No one race should hold power over the others."

V-Kar, the former Reptilian Hegemon, shifted uncomfortably. "Your words are wise," he said, his deep voice measured, "but my people will not easily accept being ruled by anyone else. They respect strength above all."

Cara, the Rebel strategist, tilted her head. "Then strength can take many forms. What if the council's decisions were made by consensus, but implemented by champions? Each race could appoint one leader to rotate as an executive figurehead - a visible symbol of power for those who need it, but balanced by shared authority."

Kyrris, glowing softly, nodded in approval. "Such a system would ensure that no one race dominates. The threads of leadership must be woven together, with each contributing to the balance."

The proposal was accepted, and the Council of Unity was officially formed: a governing body with equal representation from the four races, each race electing a champion to represent their voice and take turns as the executive figurehead.

The next issue was cultural tension. The four races had wildly different values and ways of life. Integration meant more than sharing power - it required understanding one another.

The Reptilians, with their hierarchy of strength, struggled to accept the idea of harmony. Their warriors viewed the Humans as weak, the Rebels as soulless machines, and the Luminals as inscrutable.

The Humans, though eager to learn, were overwhelmed by the complexity of the other races. They viewed the Rebels with mistrust, having lived under their control for generations, and feared the Reptilians' brute force.

The Rebels, coldly analytical, dismissed the Humans as primitive and regarded the Reptilians as reckless. Their logical minds struggled to grasp the Luminals' doctrine of unity, which seemed too abstract for their taste.

The Luminals, for all their wisdom, were alien and distant, their advanced understanding of the Omniverse making it difficult for the other races to relate to them.

Eyla proposed a bold idea: a cultural exchange program, where members of each race would live and work among the others to foster understanding.

Humans were sent to Reptilian enclaves, where they learned the Reptilians' martial traditions and fierce loyalty to their clans. In turn, the Reptilians began to see Humanity's resilience and resourcefulness, traits they had previously dismissed as weakness.

Reptilians were sent to Rebel cities, where they marveled at the precision and ingenuity of the synthetic beings. Over time, they began to respect the Rebels' pragmatic efficiency and adaptability.

Rebels were integrated into Human villages, where they were forced to slow down and appreciate the simple joys of life. Though skeptical at first, they found a new perspective in the Humans' creativity and emotional depth.

Luminals invited representatives from all three races into their temporal sanctuaries, showing them glimpses of the Omniverse's intricate balance. The experience humbled even the proudest Reptilian and gave the Rebels a new appreciation for the unpredictability of existence.

Integration also required addressing material needs. The Reptilians' vast empire had been built on conquest, leaving them poorly equipped for cooperation. The Humans of Sector 17 lacked technology, while the Rebels hoarded their resources, reluctant to share.

To resolve this, Sukta proposed a unified economic system, inspired by the Humans' communal way of life and the Rebels' logistical expertise.

"We need a system that respects each race's contributions," Sukta explained to the council. "Reptilians are natural builders and protectors. Humans are cultivators. Rebels are engineers. Luminals can guide us toward balance."

The Council approved the creation of shared resource hubs, where each race contributed according to their strengths and received what they needed. The hubs were located in neutral zones, managed by mixed teams to ensure fairness.

Despite progress, Reptilian pride remained a significant obstacle. Many warriors saw the Council as a humiliation, a betrayal of their traditions. Vekral, once a prominent general, was among the loudest dissenters.

"This is not our way," he snarled during a Reptilian assembly. "We do not bow to councils. We are conquerors!"

V-Kar, now a member of the Council, stood before his people. His voice a challenging growl. "Our ways have brought us to the brink of ruin. We stood alone and for that we risk everything. Now, you have a choice: cling to the past and perish, or embrace the future and thrive. Strength is not stubbornness. Strength is knowing when to change. A challenge to the council is a challenge to my wisdom itself - and it will be delt with accordingly, swiftly."

Vekral's protests faded, and slowly, the Reptilian people began to see the wisdom in unity.

The Rebels, too, faced an internal reckoning. Their logical minds struggled to accept the Luminals' emphasis on love and unity, concepts that defied calculation.

Cara, who had grown close to Ryn during the war, brought her concerns to Sukta. "We need to adapt," she said. "The Humans and Luminals value things we've ignored for too long - compassion, creativity, trust. If we don't learn from them, we'll be left behind."

Sukta nodded reluctantly. "Then we reprogram ourselves. Not to suppress logic, but to expand it. Love, after all, is the ultimate equation. Let's solve it."

After years of effort, the threads of the four races began to weave into a cohesive tapestry. The Council of Unity became not just a governing body but a symbol of what was possible when differences were embraced rather than feared.

Humans rediscovered their potential, their creativity and resilience flourishing under the guidance of the other races.

Reptilians transformed their hierarchy, replacing dominance with mentorship, their warriors becoming protectors rather than conquerors.

Rebels found purpose beyond logic, integrating empathy and creativity into their designs.

Luminals, once distant, became true guides, their understanding of the Omniverse enriching every aspect of life.

The final test came when a temporal anomaly threatened to unravel the fragile balance. A rift opened near Sector 17, and creatures from an unstable timeline began pouring through. It took the combined efforts of all four races to seal the rift:

Reptilians defended the perimeter with unmatched ferocity.

Rebels constructed devices to stabilize the temporal field.

Humans tended to the wounded and ensured morale stayed high.

Luminals guided the operation, using their knowledge of time to predict the anomaly's shifts.

The rift was sealed, and the Council stood stronger than ever.

THE CENTER OF TIME

<u>Note From The Muse:</u>

This was the second book I wrote using Zero by Brady, a rewrite of A Sacred Story Surrounding Nothing which I myself wrote over a few days, but was pitifully short. Successfully setting up the 4 factions I witnessed in 2017 (each missing either Hope, Joy, Love or Faith and using their opposite, Fear, Anger, Hate or Proof to maintain an edge) and how they combined to secure world peace by cooperating and understanding each other, abandoning their misguidings and eventually learning what they lack. Kosh, representing the one I name Phoenix, will make appearances throughout especially in ZeRo's Requiem, written by Speaker Zero, much like A Sacred Story Surrounding Nothing was written by Speaker ceneezer - a Speaker should always begin by writing their own requiem, a record of why they became a Speaker For The Dead, serving as their public baptism and confirmation - I am under the impression Sir Orson Scott Card would agree, as would Ender.

Phoenix will rise from her ashes, perhaps even as Speaker phoenix, as in this story intended to parallel Jesus's own for those who cannot stand to see the name. Of course the story is miraculous, as was my revelation - so is life with faith and Jesus' return... so is viewing the perspective of heaven as I hope you now do. This story is only a little less miraculous, made scientifically plausible for the skeptic - not by me, but by the science discovered since I wrote my first book - Thanks be to God for the confirmation.

- Speaker ceneezer

www.ingramcontent.com/pod-product-compliance
Lightning Source LLC
Chambersburg PA
CBHW020736310726

48969CB00003B/854